ST

大迫弘和詩集

訳 大迫明日奈

詩集　ＳＴ　＊　目次

I ひらがな

ゆうやけこやけ　8

ここから　12

なぞ　16

あした　18

きないにて　22

いちどだけ　24

いのち　26

ちきゅう　30

II ST

詩人　34

詩人、また　38

百歳の詩人に　40

挽歌　44

III　鉄腕アトム

鉄腕アトム　48

異国　52

残り時間　54

名づけられないものたち　56

道　58

奇跡　62

IV　Sharing the Planet

兵士独白　66

贖罪　68

舞台　70

襤褸　72

言い伝え　74

ルージュ　76

語り部ばばあ　78

V　諸相

見果てぬ夢　82

シアターX　86

わたしは Camille　88

EIGHTEEN　90

辞表　92

主体的な死　96

ゼッケン　98

あとがき　谷川俊太郎さんのこと　100

ST（英訳）　168

詩集

S
T

I

ひらがな

ゆうやけこやけ

こどもが
みちを
あるいてる
ゆうやけこやけの
そらのした
こどもが
みちで
けんかする

ゆうやけこやけの
そらのした

こどもが
やんまを
おいかける
ゆうやけこやけの
そらのした

こどもが
こいしを
うちゅうになげる
ゆうやけこやけの
そらのした

こどもが
いつか
おもいだす
ともといっしょの
ゆうやけこやけの
そらのした

ここから

ここは
どこかに
いけるばしょ
そこがどこかは
わからない

でも
もしきみがのぞむなら
かならずどこかに

いけるばしょ

とてもとおく
かもしれない
とてもちかく
かもしれない
でもそこは
ここではない
きみが
ここから
むかうばしょ

そのばしょで
きっときみは

いのるはず

せかいじゅうのひとたちが

みんなしあわせになりますように

いまからきみは

そんなところへ

むかうんだ

ここから

そこに

むかうんだ

なぞ

ぜったいとけない
なぞがある
だから
ひとは
かんがえる

ぜったいそれは
わからない
だから
ひとは

しりたくなる

なぜ
うまれてきたのだろう
なぜ
うまれてきたら
しぬまでいきるのだろう

ぜったいとけない
なぞがある
たぶん
それは
いきていくための
なぞなんだ

あした

わからなくなっちゃった
さんすうのけいさんは
だいじょうぶなんだけど

わからなくなっちゃった
とおくのやまなみは
かわらないんだけど

あしたのあさ

めがさめて
いちにちが
はじまる

だけど
どうして
あしたのなかに
ぼくがいるんだろう
ぼくがいなくても
あしたは
はじまっていくのに

ぼくに
わからなくなっちゃった

どうして
あしたがあるの

だけど
あさになったら
あしたも
ぼくは
おきる

できたらじぶんで
おきてみる
あしたが
ぼくに
いっている

わからなくなっちゃったんならそうしなさい

きないにて

うつくしいことを
かきたい
いま
ひこうきのなか

うつくしいことを
かきたい
ふじさんが
みえる

うつくしいことを
かきたい

きっと

ひらがなが

よい

うつくしいことを
かきたい
うつくしいことだけを
かきたい
てんごくにいくのがたのしみという
たったひとりの
あなたのために

いちどだけ

たったいちどの
じんせい
おいしいものを
ちゅうもんする

たったいちどの
じんせい
わかれたあなたを
おもいだす

たったいちどの
じんせい
いくつかのしを
かいた

たったいちどの
じんせい
いちどきりが
いとおしい

いのち

あなたのことを
いのっているのに
すくわれるのは
わたし
それは
なぜ
いのりって
そういうものなの？

あなたを
あいでみたしたいのに
あいでみたされていくのは
わたし
それは
なぜ
あいって
そういうものなの？

あなたと
ずっといっしょにいたいのに
あなたよりさきに
わたしがしんでしまう
それは

なぜ
いのちって
そういうものなの？

ちきゅう

そんなふうに
ひとが
ひとを
にくむなんて
このちきゅうのうえで

そんなふうに
ひとが
ひとから

うばうなんて
このちきゅうのうえで

そんなふうに
ひとが
ひとを
ころすなんて
このちきゅうのうえで

あいしあうために
うまれてきたはずの
この
ちきゅうの
うえで

Ⅱ

S
T

詩人

詩人は
詩人でなくなるために
詩を書き続けました

詩人は
ことばを疑いながら
詩を書き続けました

詩人は

いつか詩が詩でなくなることを夢見て

詩を書き続けました

詩人は

誰よりも黙っていたかったですが

そのためには

どうしても詩を書かなくてはならなくて

だれよりも多くの詩を書き続けました

詩人の最後の詩を

誰よりも一番楽しみにしていたのは

言うまでもなく

詩人自身であったのでしたが

詩人はそれに出会うことがないことを

詩を書き続けるのでした
うすうす気づきながら
それは詩人の
詩人としての運命でした
そして
詩人は
その運命を
だれよりも愛しているのでした

（詩集『ルリビタキ』より）

詩人、また

言葉が
そう言って詩人は朽ちた
ベトナムの戦場で
農婦に銃を放てなかった兵士のように

愛を
そう言って詩人は黙した
ある日突然
右手が動かなくなったピアニストのように

宇宙へ
そう言って詩人は部屋を出ていった
Ｔシャツを着たまま
父母の写真の飾られた木製の部屋を

Farewellではない
僕らの詩人よ
あなたが遠くの人になることは
永遠にない

（詩集『ルリビタキ』より）

百歳の詩人に

あなたは
わたくしたちにとって
すでに永遠の存在であり
ですからわたくしたちにとって
あなたの年齢は
もはや意味をなさないのです

詩人になるために生まれてきたあなたが書いた詩は
世界に屹立し

それらが
わたくしたちを
ここまでかろうじて生き続けさせ
今日まであなたの詩とともにあったことを
わたしたちは
なによりの人生的価値と思っています

あなたのバースデーに
杉並のご自宅に
お祝いをお届けしたい気持ちもありますが
お祝いの気持ち以上の
何か崇高で
とても透明な気持ちを
あなたのお誕生日が

わたくしたちに
呼び起こしてくれるのです

その気持ちは
まるでイエスキリストが
わたくしたちの罪を一身に背負い
すすんで十字架に磔にされたように
あなたの詩が
わたくしたちの
穢れを
一身に
引き受けてくださっているためなのでしょう

百歳のその日

あなたが書く詩のことが
明日の遠足のように
ただ楽しみで
今夜は眠れそうにありません

Happy　Birthday！

（詩集『ルリビタキ』より）

挽歌

谷川さんも死ぬんだ

谷川さんは死なないと思ってた

でも谷川さんも死ぬんだ

谷川さんの40代を知っている

僕は東大生だった

渋谷のジャンジャンだった

その日

僕は

谷川俊太郎は死なないと思った
そのくらいTシャツの胸板は厚く肉感に満ち
あの少し高音の早口の言葉たちに
この人は死なないと思った
僕は思った
僕の詩を魂から生まれる言葉と言って下さった
ご自宅で話せるようになり
だから
谷川さんは死なない
天に召された13日の夜に
メディアが谷川さんの死を伝える今日
息が苦しくなる夢で
魘されたことを

谷川さんが来たからだとは思わない

谷川さんは
死なない
そのことは
誰にもゆずらない

（2024年11月19日）

III
鉄腕アトム

鉄腕アトム

はじめて夢の中で詩を書いていた
71歳になった朝のことだ
71歳になった僕が鉄腕アトムに会うという詩だった
空をこえて　ららら　って知ってる？
と鉄腕アトムに聞くと
知ってるよと鉄腕アトムは答えた
いつまでたっても君は年をとらないねというめちゃくちゃ陳腐な
一言を僕が発する

母が横で僕の詩を盗み見していた

僕は一直線という言葉を直線的にという言葉に変えるために

一直線を鉛筆で消した

母はその書き直しを見ていた

僕は次に可逆的、非可逆的という言葉を思い浮かべていた

おそらく人生の流れに関して

いずれにせよ

詩と言えないことばたちばかり

それでも

僕は詩を書いていた

詩人になるのに71年かかった

23歳で死んでいたら

僕は

詩人になれなかった

僕が詩人であるかどうかを決めるのは僕ではなく

あなたが僕を詩人と思ってくれるなら僕は詩人だ

あなたが

夢の中で

僕を詩人にする

71歳の朝

（2024年10月6日　朝）

異国

ことばのようなもので
あいのようなものを
わたしのようなだれかが
あなたに語ろうとしていた

それは本当にことばだったのだろうか
それは本当にあいだったのだろうか
それは本当にわたしだったのだろうか

わたしのいのちが出ていこうとする
あなたに向かって出ていこうとする

あなたに向かいながら
わたしはわたしの不在を確かめる
あなたに不在を告げるように
わたしを確かめるわたしがわたしの不在を確かめる

わたしがゆるやかに
とけていく

ことばもあいもあなたも
もしかしたらわたしも
もういらなく思える
異国での
目覚めのような
不在

残り時間

ことばがあるような気がする
もうすぐそこにあるような気がする
ずっと探していた
あなたへのことばが

ことばを探した
ことばだけを探した
ひっくり返して探した
しかしすべてが違っていた

もう一度探した
そのようにして今日までがあった

私にはあとどのくらい時間が残されているのだろうか
そのことばに行きつくための時間が

もしかしたら
どこにもないかもしれない
あなたのためのそのことばに
私は最後に
行きつくことができるだろうか
空の匂いを嗅ぎながら

名づけられないものたち

私の中の名づけられないものたちが
空の向こうに向かっていく
空の向こうに向かうことにより
名づけられることを願うかのように

リベンジのように
あなたの中の名づけられないものたちが
私の中に向かってくる
私はそれを悲しいくらい貪欲に

私の空洞に注ぎ込む

だが
それら
すべては
この世では名づけられず
許されないものになり
それゆえに
美しい形になっていく

私の言葉の位置を決めたのは
私ではない

道

風わたる竹林
風に吹かれ
道が続く

風つづく道
風と行くことの
清々しさ

あの日

あなたは舞い
風になった
そのとき
わたしはわたしのいのちを忘れ
わたしはわたしの名を忘れた

わたしはわたしにさいなまれたわたしを忘れた

風になったあなたが
わたしのいのちを呼び
わたしの名を呼んだ
あなたはただ舞っただけ

風わたり続け

道どこまでも続く

あなたの生とわたしの生は
あなたとわたしのものになり
あなたとわたしは風に結ばれる
遠い日に
歩いた道を
もう一度歩くようにしながら

奇跡

あなたには許されるという幻想が
わたしを許せないわたしが
そのままわたしが終わろうとも
わたしはわたしを許せない
そうであっても
奇跡の許しがある
あの方はわたしを許す
わたしはわたしを許せない

わたしたちを支えた時間だったのだろうか

そろそろ終わりが近づいてきたわたしたちの時間とは

わたしはわたしを許せず

そのようであっても

あなたに許されたわたしがあった

それは幻想ではなかった

そのようなわたしたちの時間は

たしかにあったのだと

そもそも

すべてが

奇跡だったのだと

あなたは

その時

わたしに
そのように言ってくれるだろうか
世界の美しさがそこにあったと

IV

Sharing the Planet

兵士独白

ウクライナってどこにあるのだろう

僕は今からそこに向かう

戦争に参加するために

なぜなら

僕は

兵士だから

僕はそこでウクライナの人を殺すのだろう

意味は分からない

でも

僕は

兵士だから

命令が下された

君たちは

明日

ウクライナへ向かう

ウクライナって

どこにあるのだろう

贖罪

学校はいつも間違いだらけだ
それでも先生がいて
子どもたちは先生を信じて
大きくなる

先生が正しいなんて嘘だ
迷う人だ
それでも子どもたちは
大きくなる

先生よ
あなたは子どもたちの前で時代を演じさせられた
哀しい歯車だったのですね

再び
学校が

贖罪の場になりませんように

（2024年8月15日　79回目の終戦の日に）

舞台

私たちがゆっくり死んでいくように

地球もゆっくり死んでいく

私たちに死期を早める生き方があるように

地球の死期が早まることもある

私たちがあの日に戻れないように

地球もあの日には戻れない

私たちに人生の舞台があるように

地球にも生命の舞台がある

西暦2024年

地球の舞台

汗ばむ日本

襤褸

哲学書を読む人はもういない
いつか書物というものもなくなるかもしれない

太陽がなくなる前に
ヒトがいなくなるかもしれない

失いへの努力は潰え
物語はもう始まらない

愛と信頼と勇気が
無人の地球の
襤褸となる

言い伝え

本というものがあったらしい

紙というものでできていて

手に持って読んだということだ

タバコというものがあったらしい

乾いた植物に火をつけて

手で口に運んだということだ

愛というものがあったらしい

見つめ合い
手のぬくみを確かめ合ったということだ

ルージュ

物質というルージュが施された地球

眠る前にも
落とせないルージュ

もっと派手に
もっと淫らに

老婆が呟く
後悔するよ

すっぴんのほうがきれいなのに

少女たちは
小枝のようなルージュを
コンビニで万引きする

語り部ばばあ

原爆はな
とばばあは言う
悲劇のほんのはじまりだった
そのあとにな
その60年くらいあとにな
四角いものが現れてな
世界は滅びにむかったんだ
そいつにな

人間は吸い取られちまったんだ
人間はな
四六時中そいつをな
そいつだけを見とった
片時も離さずにな
それですべてはおわっちまったんだ

そういうことがあったけなぁ

V

諸
相

見果てぬ夢

いつまで歌うの
いつまでも歌って

いつまで真っ赤な薔薇の色のドレスを着るの
いつまでも着て

いつまで平和を語るの
いつまでも語って

いつまで愛を伝えるの
いつまでも伝えて

それがあなただって
だからあなただって

ほら

今日も
会場はいっぱい

鬼武さんのピアノが流れる
あなたが
ステージに現れる
光の粒に包まれて

あなたは歌い始める
あなたが愛したあの人と
今も
見果てぬ夢を
追いかけて

──加藤登紀子さんへ──

シアターX

あなたの中に入りたい
Eros ではなく
もっとあどけない形で
ひとつになっても
ひとつでない形で

哀しさを少しだけ忘れることができる
そのための舞台が
化粧と意匠で 魔性を生む

あなたの科白は
まるでいやいやながら呼吸するようだ
母国と祖国と日本国に引き裂かれながら
観客に問う
「もうやめる?」と
何度も何度も「もうやめる?」と
おそらくそれは
あなた自身への問いだ
ましてや問いなど
照明も音響もなければよいね
化粧を落とせなかった使い古しの台本が一冊
ポツリと楽屋の鏡の中にいた

　　　　―女優Kへ―

わたしは Camille

愛の本質は切なさとときめきなんだと

知った風なことを言うじゃない

何も分かっていないくせに

これは今までと違うんだと

もう何人にも言っていることは知っている

信じている振りはしてあげるけど

あなたのどこが好きになったかは教えてあげない

だけど

切なさは息ができなくなるくらいに苦しくて

あなたが本当は一度も体験したことがないことなんだってことは

いつか教えてあげたいとは思ってる

わたしはもうなにもつくらないと決めたわ

―Rodin へ―

EIGHTEEN

18歳だと17歳より幸せになれるのかなぁ

人間ってだんだん幸せになれるのかなぁ

それとも

人間ってだんだんだめになってくのかなぁ

私の肌は多分まだ綺麗

だってママのより綺麗だもの

でも

いつかママみたいになるのかなぁ

さかさまの絵を描いた
そうしたら
地面に虹が見えた
それが私の18歳のバースデーの出来事

明日は
今日より
のどが渇きそう

―ライバーYへ―

辞表

僕は僕を辞めたい
一身上の都合で

辞表はどこに出せばよいのか
形式は自由か
自筆でなければだめか

僕を辞めて
さあどうなる

僕に次はあるか
ハローワークはややこしそうだ

辞表を胸に
改札口を抜け
階段を上がり
ホームに出て
山手線に乗る

どうやらまだ僕のままだ
だれかが僕を見ている
次の駅で降りよう
あなたに会うために

山手線が

少し

揺れた

主体的な死

主体的に
死を迎えたいと
そう思う

主体的とはなんぞや
定義が曖昧な言葉の一つであろう
だがそもそも定義ができると考えるのが過ちだと
そう思う

だが
主体的に死を迎えたいとなると
主体的ということが
一気に詳らかになるのではないかと
そう思う

たった一人で死んでいく
おそらくその時あなたのことを思うかもしれないが
わたしの心臓と脳波は止まり
わたしの生が閉じられる
それが主体的であるということだと
そう思う

ゼッケン

地下鉄の中でのことだ
向かい側の座席に幸せそうな家族が座っている
お兄ちゃんと妹とママは胸にゼッケンをつけたまま
市民マラソン大会の帰り道なのだろう
パパはとても健康そうだがゼッケンをつけていない
お兄ちゃんと妹はマラソン大会の賞品がわんさと詰まった袋から
お菓子をパクパク
マラソン大会のスポンサーがあれもこれも詰め込む様子が
思い浮かぶ

お兄ちゃんは将来はマラソン選手になり

妹はどうするかな

いまはお兄ちゃんのやることはなんでも真似するけど

わたしは

座席で眠くなっていく

このまま眠って眠ったまま

このまま死んでしまうのは気持ちがよさそうだ

目を閉じると

幸せなゼッケンが

次第に遠退いていくのでした

あとがき　谷川俊太郎さんのこと

　京都の同志社は大学附属の小学校を二つ持っていて、その一つの小学校の校歌は谷川さんが作詞した「えらい人になるよりも　よい人間になりたいな」、もう一つの国際小学校の校歌は私が作詞しています（「よいこころのひとになるために」作曲は小椋佳さん）。それはご縁ということになるかもしれませんが、私にとって谷川俊太郎さんはそのようなご縁をはるかに超えた本当に特別な存在でした。

　NHKのお昼の番組でした。そこで谷川さんの朗読を初めて聞きました。それは私が作詞していました大学生の時でした。

　　本当のことを言おうか
　　詩人のふりはしているが
　　私は詩人ではない

　その朗読の衝撃は私の人生にとって決定的なものでした。50年前のことです。

（『鳥羽　1』）

何年もの後、ご自宅をお訪ねしてお話をさせていただくようになり、本当に色々なことを教えていただきました。谷川さんからプレゼントをいただくこともありました。最初にいただいたのがマヤコフスキーの『ミステリヤ・ブッフ』の日本語版の本（土曜社）で谷川さんが序文を書いていたものでした。私が大学でロシア文学を学んでいたということを話したので、それなら大迫さんにはこれがいいのではと選んでくださったのだと思います。

子どもたちのための詩や絵本の朗読の動画をご自宅で二人で制作したこともありました。一時間くらいの動画が出来上がりました。その時、私が書いた台本の一部です。

番号		内容
7	詩「さようなら」（『はだか』から）朗読	英語テロップを挿入 可能ならDVD「詩人　谷川俊太郎」に収録されている歌唱を挿入
8	『ことばあそびうた』から最初の「のはな」「やんま」「き」「かっぱ」「うそつきつつき」「ばか」「いるか」の7編を連続朗読	画面に各ページを映し出す このパートは日本語の音を楽しむことを主眼に英語はなし

10	9
子どもたちからのいくつかの質問	『ことばあそびうた』に関するお話
事前に子どもたちの質問を集めておく 当日、箱に入れ、谷川さんに無作為に引いていただく（あるいは事前に質問を一応全部見ていただく必要がありますか？　即興の方が面白い？）	大迫がMC

その時、谷川さんが朗読に使われた詩集は『はだか』も『ことばあそびうた』も、その他の詩集もすべて私が持っていたもので、谷川さんは「なんでも持っているんだねぇ」と楽しそうにからかい気味に言われたのでした。今、谷川さんの手の温もりが残っているそれらの詩集をなによりも大切にしています。

この動画の制作の前に、子どもたちが谷川さんの詩を朗読する様子を撮影して見ていただきました。谷川さんはそれをご覧になって子どもたちにお返事を書いてくださいました。

『私の詩を読んでくれてありがとう。活字が声になると生きものになるね。』『私の詩を読んでくれてありがとう。みんなの声を聞いていると自分の詩が自分のものでなく

なってみんなのものになったような気がします。」

本詩集『ST』には2023年4月に上梓した『ルリビタキ』より「詩人」「詩人、また」「百歳の詩人に」を収めました。その他の詩は新しい詩になります。

『ルリビタキ』に谷川俊太郎さんは次のような序を書いてくださいました。

魂から生まれる言葉

谷川俊太郎

「樹」と題された詩の始まりを読んだとき、あれ？こんなの変だと思った人もいるかもしれません。「樹はすべてを知っている／樹は何も知らない」普通の文ではこんな真逆なことは書きませんよね。でも詩ではこういう矛盾した言葉が読者の脳を刺激し、今まで気づかなかったより深い現実に目覚めさせることがあります。そのためにはこれまで教わってきたこと、知っていることをいったん白紙に戻してみることが必要です。

「なんにもないということが／そこにあるということだ」詩は時にマジックです。だまされることで世界の見方が変わってきます。そこに新しい真実があるということを信じて、詩人は書くのです。大迫さんの詩は魂から生まれてきます。詩は人間の理性、知性、感性が創るものですが、大迫さんの詩はそれらよりももっと深い、それ故に時に理解が難しい魂から生まれてきます。

大迫さんの言う〈あなた〉は人間のあなたと同時に人間のあなたを超えた存在に向けられています。それを簡単に〈神〉という言葉で呼んでしまわないところにも、詩を書く大迫さんの魂のありかを感じます。

多くの人たちの心の中に谷川俊太郎さんが今もいます。多くの人たちが谷川俊太郎さんを、そしてその作品を愛しています。谷川俊太郎さんと出会い、導かれ、世界が広がった人たちが溢れるほどいると思います。その中のほんの一人としてこの詩集を書きました。ほんの一人であると思うのですが、本当に嬉しかった谷川さんの言葉を書かせていただきます。谷川さんがある方に私のことを紹介する時に、私のことを「古くからの詩の仲間」と言ってくださったのでした。身に余る光栄でした。私の人生の中で最も嬉しかった瞬間でした。

また別の時に、私が「私はいちファンに過ぎません」と申し上げた時に「大迫さんはファンの中でもトップファイブに入るよ」と笑顔で言ってくださったことも楽しい思い出です。

気持ちとしてはこの詩集を早く形にしたかったので土曜美術社出版販売の髙木祐子さんに心から感謝しています。

2024年11月30日

大迫弘和

谷川俊太郎さんと　2020年8月20日（ご自宅にて）

著者略歴

大迫弘和 （おおさこ・ひろかず）

日本を代表する教育者の一人。現在海城中学高等学校校長。
詩人としても活動。作品に『がっこう』（2012年　かまくら春秋社）、『定義以前』（2017年　遊行社）、『木漏れ陽』（2019年　メッセージデザインセンター）等多数。
東京大学文学部卒。

大迫明日奈 （おおさこ・あすな）

翻訳家、詩人の娘。
サイコセラピスト、ニューヨーク在住。
gentledepththerapy.com
コロンビア大学大学院卒、臨床社会福祉学修士号取得。

詩集　ST

発　行　二〇二五年四月一日

著　者　大迫弘和

装　幀　直井和夫

発行者　高木祐子

発行所　土曜美術社出版販売
〒162-0813　東京都新宿区東五軒町三─一〇
電　話　〇三─五二二九─〇七三〇
FAX　〇三─五二二九─〇七三二
振　替　〇〇一六〇─九─七五六九〇九

印刷・製本　モリモト印刷
DTP　直井デザイン室

ISBN978-4-8120-2892-6　C0092

© Osako Hirokazu 2025, Printed in Japan

I start to feel drowsy
in my seat.
I bet it would feel good to fall asleep
and drift away into death as I sleep.

As I close my eyes,
the happiness-filled bibs
gradually fade away.

Number Bibs

It was inside of the subway—
I saw, sitting across from me, a happy-looking
    family.
Brother, younger sister, and Mom, all still wearing
    number bibs,
probably on their way home from the city
    marathon.
Dad looked healthy but wasn't wearing a bib.
Brother and sister gobbling down snacks
out of the prize-stuffed bags from the marathon
    event.
The image of the sponsors stuffing the bags full
    comes to mind.

The older brother may become a marathon runner
    in the future.
I wonder what the little sister will do.
For now, she just copies everything her brother
    does.

That is what it is to be autonomous.
That's what I think.

An Autonomous Death

I would like to meet death
autonomously.
That's what I think.

What the heck does "autonomously" mean?
It is one of those words with an ambiguous
     definition.
But it's a mistake to believe it's definable to
     begin with.
That's what I think.

But
If you can meet death autonomously,
Then I suspect that the meaning of autonomous
will suddenly become clear.
That's what I think.

I will die alone.
Perhaps I will think of you when that time comes,
but my heart and brain waves will stop
and my life will come to an end.

To go and see you.

The Yamonote Line,
Slightly
Shook.

Resignation Letter

I want to quit myself.
For personal reasons.

Where should I submit my resignation letter?
Is the format freeform?
Does it need to be handwritten?

What will happen if I quit myself?
Is there a "next" for me?
The Employment Service Center seems very
    complicated.

With my resignation in my pocket
I pass through the station gate,
climb up the stairs,
step onto the platform,
and board the Yamanote Line.

It seems I am still me.
Someone is looking at me.
I should get off at the next station

Eighteen

Will I be happier at 18 than I am at 17?
Do people gradually become happier and happier?
Or
Do people gradually become no good?

I will probably still have good skin,
because my skin is better than Mom's.
But
Will I become like Mom someday?

I drew an up-side-down picture
And then
Saw a rainbow on the ground.
This was the event of my 18th birthday.

Tomorrow
I think I'll be more thirsty
than I was today.

(To Influencer Y)

I am Camille

"The essence of love is longing and excitement,"
you say, as if you know,
Even though you don't understand a thing.

"This is different from anything I've experienced."
I know you've said the same thing to so many,
Even though I pretend to believe you.

I won't tell you what, about you, I fell in love with.
But
One day I plan to tell you that
You've never actually experienced—not once—
A true longing that makes it hard, even to breathe.

I have decided, I will no longer create anything

(To Rodin)

It would be better if there were no lighting
        or sound,
Let alone questions.
A single worn out script that couldn't remove
        its makeup
Sat alone inside the dressing room mirror.

                                    (To Actress K)

Theatre X

I want to enter you.
Not in an Eros way.
In an innocent form—
where we are not one
even as we become one.

I can forget my sadness a little.
The stage creating a demonic allure
through makeup and design.

Your lines
breathed out, almost reluctantly.
Torn apart between homeland, motherland, and
    Japan,
You ask the audience,
"Do you want to quit?"
Again and again asking, "Do you want to quit?"
The question probably
directed towards yourself.

You begin to sing.
The one you loved still within,
Continuing to chase
Your unfinished dream.

(To Tokiko Kato)

An Unfinished Dream

How long will you sing?
Please sing forever.

How long will you wear that bright rose-red dress?
Please wear it forever.

How long will you speak of peace?
Please speak of it forever.

How long will you express love?
Please express it forever.

That is who you are.
That is why you are.
See, look,
Even today,
The music hall is full.

Ms. Onitake's piano flows.
You appear on the stage,
Enveloped by glittering lights.

V Various Aspects

The Storytelling Crone

"That atomic bomb,"
said the crone,
"was merely the start to the tragedy, you see.
After that—about 60 years after—
this rectangular thing appeared, you see,
and it drove the world into ruin.

This thing
sucked human beings in, you see.
People would spend 24/7,
staring only at this thing.
Not letting go, you see.
Not only for a moment.
And with that, everything ended.

What a thing that was…"

Rouge

The Earth, adorned with a material called rouge
Rouge that can't be removed,
even before sleep

More gaudy
More lewd

The old woman mummers
"You'll regret it.
You're prettier without makeup."

Young girls shoplift
twig-like rouge
from the convenience store

Folklore

I heard tell there once was a thing called "books,"
made with something called "paper."
It was held in one's hands and read.

I heard tell there was once a thing called
    "cigarettes,"
where dried-up plants were lit on fire
and brought to one's mouth with one's hand.

I heard tell that there was once a thing called
    "love,"
where people would gaze at each other
and reassure each other through the warmth of
    their hands.

Rags

Noone reads philosophy books anymore.
One day, books themselves may no longer exist.

Before the sun becomes extinct,
Humans may no longer exist.

The efforts to prevent loss are crushed.
No new stories will ever be born.

Love, trust, and courage,
Turning into rags
on a desolate earth.

Stage

Just as we slowly die
the Earth slowly dies, too

Just as there are ways of living that hasten
　　our death
the Earth's death can also be hastened

Just as we cannot go back to that day
the Earth cannot go back to that day either

Just as our lives take place on a stage
the Earth too exists on a stage

Year 2024
On the Earth's stage
Japan sweats

Atonement

Schools are full of mistakes.
Even so, there are teachers,
and the children grow up
trusting those teachers.

It is a lie that teachers are right.
They are torn by doubt.
Despite this,
children still grow up.

O teachers,
You were but mere pawns of the times,
forced to act in front of the children.

May schools
Never again
Become a place of atonement.

> (On August 15, 2024,
> the 79th commemoration of the end of the war)

Soldier's Monologue

I wonder where Ukraine is.
I am heading there now
to fight in the war
because
I am a soldier.

I will probably kill Ukrainians there,
although I don't know why,
but
because
I am a soldier.

Orders are out.
"You will
head to Ukraine
tomorrow."

Where is Ukraine…
I wonder.

IV Sharing the Planet

When the time comes,
will you speak those words to me?
That there lay the beauty of the world.

Miracle

I cannot forgive myself,
but He forgives me.
A miraculous forgiveness.
But even still,
I cannot forgive myself—
probably until the end of my days.

Was the support I felt during the time we had
—time that is now nearing an end—
based on the fantasy that you will forgive me
even though I cannot forgive myself?

I could not forgive myself,
yet you forgave me,
and I existed as someone you forgave.
Will you tell me
that the time we had was not a fantasy,
but real?
That, from the very beginning,
everything
was a miracle.

Your life and my life become our own
You and I are bound together by the wind
As we walk once again
the path we once walked
in days of a distant past

Path

A windswept bamboo forest
Blown by the wind
The path goes on

An ever windy road
Going along with the wind
Brisk and invigorating

That day you danced and became the wind
In that moment I forgot my own life
and forgot my own name

I forgot the self that I had tormented

You, as the wind
called forth my life
and called forth my name
even though you only danced

The wind blows on
The path stretches on forever

The Things That Can't Be Named

The things within me that can't be named
head towards the sky.
As if wishing that
by going towards the sky,
they will be named.

Almost like revenge,
the things within you that can't be named
head towards me.
I greedily pour them in, almost to a pathetic degree,
to the hollow space inside me.

However,
in this world,
none of these things are named
and become unforgivable things;
hence,
take on a beautiful form.

It is not I,
who decided the placement of my words.

The Time Left

I feel the words are there.
It feels like they're just out of reach.
The words I've been looking for—
the ones I want to send to you.

I looked for the words.
I looked only for the words.
I flipped things over, looking,
but they were all wrong.
I tried looking again.
In this way, I have come to today.

I wonder how much time I have left
to be able to arrive at those words.

Perhaps they don't
exist anywhere at all.
Will I ultimately arrive
at those words for you
at the very end?
While breathing in the scent of the sky.

Words, love, you,
and perhaps even me
are no longer necessary.
Absent—
as if waking up
in a foreign country.

Foreign Country

Using something like words,
A person something like me,
Was trying to express to you,
Something like love.

Were those really words?
Was that really love?
Was that really me?

My life force is trying to flow out
Trying to flow out towards you.
As I head towards you,
I make sure of my own absence.
Just as I alert you of my absence
The 'me' that confirms my absence
     makes sure of my absence.

I gently
Melt away.

I was still writing poems.

It took me 71 years to become a poet.
If I had died at age 23
I would never have become a poet.
I am not the one who gets to decide whether I am a
        poet or not.
If you think of me as a poet, then I am a poet.

You turn me into a poet
Inside a dream
The morning I turn 71.

(The morning of October 6th, 2024)

Astro Boy

On the morning I turned 71,
I dreamed for the first time that I was writing a
     poem:
A poem about my 71-year-old self meeting Astro
     Boy.
"Do you know the song 'Beyond the sky, la-la-la?'"
I asked Astro Boy.
"Yes, of course," he replied.
I make a super cliche remark, "You never age, do
     you?"

Beside me, my mother was peeking at my poem.
I scratched out the word "straight" with a pencil to
     replace it with the word "linearly."
My mother was watching my revision.
Next, I was thinking of the words "reversible" and
     "irreversible"
Likely regarding the flow of life.
In any case,
they were all words that can't be considered poetry.
Nevertheless,

Ⅲ   Astro Boy

That's why,
even as the media reports today
that he was called to heaven on the night of
   the 13th,
I refuse to believe that the
dream I had where I struggled to breathe
was because Tanikawa-san came to me.

Tanikawa-san will never die.
I will not yield this to anyone.

(November 19, 2024)

*Shibuya Jean-Jean: A small, iconic theater located in Shibuya, Tokyo, known for hosting renowned artists and performances. It was open from 1969 to 2000 and was a significant venue in the Japanese art and performance scene during its time.

Elegy

Tanikawa-san dies too.
I thought Tanikawa-san wouldn't die.
But Tanikawa-san dies too.

I know how Tanikawa-san was in his 40s.
I was a Tokyo University student then.
It was at *Shibuya Jean-Jean**.
On that day
I thought to myself,
Shuntaro Tanikawa will not die.
His T-shirt stretched taut across a broad, solid
     chest,
words flowing quickly in his slightly higher voice.
I thought, *this person will never die.*

We became close enough that I could visit and talk
     with him at his home.
He graciously told me that my poems were words
     born from the soul.
I thought,
Tanikawa-san will never die.

This feeling is probably because
your poems,
much like Jesus Christ
willingly dying on the cross to bear our sins,
fully bears
our impurities.

I'm filled with excitement for the poem you
    will write
on the day you turn one hundred.
Like a child
eagerly anticipating the next day's field trip,
I don't think I'll be able to sleep tonight.

Happy Birthday!

(From the poetry book *Ruribitaki*)

To the Hundred-Year-Old Poet

To us
you are already
an eternal presence.
So, your age
no longer holds meaning for us.

The poems written by you, who were born
        to be a poet,
stand tall in the world,
helping us survive to this point.
Being able to live
alongside your poems until today
has given such value to our lives.

On your birthday,
I would like to send you well wishes
to your home in Suginami.
But your birthday evokes within us
something much more ethereal and pure
than simply celebratory feelings.

The Poet, Again

"The words!"
said the Poet, and then withered away.
Just like the soldier who wasn't able
to shoot the peasant woman in the Vietnam War.

"Love!"
said the Poet, and then went silent.
Just like the pianist who one day
suddenly lost the ability to move his right hand.

"To space!"
said the Poet, and then left the room;
the wooden room with the photo of his parents,
still wearing his T-shirt.

This is not farewell,
Dear Poet of ours.
You will never become distant to us.
Not ever.

(From the poetry book *Ruribitaki*)

It goes without saying that
the Poet himself was the person
most excited for the Poet's final poem.
But as he gradually came to realize
that this would never come to be,
the Poet continually wrote poems.

This was the Poet's destiny
as a poet.
And
the Poet
loved this destiny
more than anyone.

(From the poetry book *Ruribitaki*)

The Poet

In order to no longer be a poet,
the Poet
continued to write poems.

Doubting words along the way,
the Poet
continued to write poems.

Dreaming of the day his poems would cease
    being poetry,
the Poet
continued to write poems.

The Poet
wanted to be silent more than anyone.
But for that to happen,
needed to write poems,
so he continued to write
more poems than anyone.

II ST

earth

The way
people hate
each other...
on the face of this earth

The way
people take
from each other...
on the face of this earth

The way
people kill
each other...
on the face of this earth

Though we were meant
to love each other.
On the
face of
this earth.

life

I pray for you...
yet I'm the one
who is saved.
Why is this?
Why is prayer
this way?

I want to fill you with love...
yet I'm the one
who gets filled with love.
Why is this?
Why is love
this way?

I want to stay with you forever...
yet I'm the one
who dies before you.
Why is this?
Why is life
this way?

only once

In this one and
only life,
I order
delicious food.

In this one and
only life,
I think of you,
the one I bid farewell to.

In this one and
only life,
I wrote
a few poems.

In this one and
only life,
I treasure its fleetingness—
only once.

*Hiragana: the basic Japanese phonetic alphabet, used to represent all the sounds in the Japanese language. It is one of the three writing systems in Japanese, alongside katakana and kanji. The term "hiragana" means "common" or "simple" kana, in contrast to the more complex kanji.

from the plane

I want to write
something beautiful.
I am in the airplane now.

I want to write
something beautiful.
I can see Mt. Fuji.

I want to write
something beautiful.
Hiragana* is probably best.

I want to write
something beautiful.
I want to write
only beautiful things.
Only for you,
who say you look forward
to going to heaven.

I've become confused.
Why does tomorrow
exist for me?

Yet
when morning comes,
I will wake again tomorrow.
If I can,
I'll try to wake up
on my own.
Tomorrow is saying to me,
"If you've become confused,
that's what you should do."

tomorrow

I've become confused.
Even though
I can still do arithmetics.

I've become confused.
Even though the mountain ranges in the distance
are unchanged.

Tomorrow morning
I will wake
and a new day
will start.

But why do I exist
within tomorrow?
Even though
tomorrow exists
and starts
without me.

mystery

There is a mystery
that can never be solved.
That's why
people think about this or that.

It is something
that can never be known.
That's why
people want to know.

Why are we born?
Why do we live until we die,
once we are born?

There is a mystery
that can never be solved.
That mystery
is probably there
for us to live.

In that place,
you will surely pray
for the happiness
of all of humanity.

Starting now,
you are going
towards that kind of place.
From this place,
you will go.

from this place

This place is a place
from where
you can go places.
You don't know
to where yet.

But as long as you will it,
this is a place
from where
you will go places.

You might go
very far away.
You might stay
very close by.
But that place
will not be here.
A new place,
where you will go
from here.

under the
sunset glow sky

children will
one day recall
the days spent
together with friends
under the
sunset glow sky

sunset glow sky

children are
walking
down the path
under the
sunset glow sky

children are
arguing
on the path
under the
sunset glow sky

children are
chasing
large dragonflies
under the
sunset glow sky

children toss
pebbles
into outer space

I Hiragana

Ⅳ Sharing the Planet

Soldier's Monologue   127

Atonement   126

Stage   125

Rags   124

Folklore   123

Rouge   122

The Storytelling Crone   121

Ⅴ Various Aspects

An Unfinished Dream   119

Theatre X   117

I am Camille   115

Eighteen   114

Resignation Letter   113

An Autonomous Death   111

Number Bibs   109

Table of Contents

I Hiragana

sunset glow sky   163

from this place   161

mystery   159

tomorrow   157

from the plane   155

only once   153

life   152

earth   151

II ST

The Poet   149

The Poet, Again   147

To the Hundred-Year-Old Poet   145

Elegy   143

III Astro Boy

Astro Boy   139

Foreign Country   137

The Time Left   135

The Things That Can't Be Named   134

Path   133

Miracle   131

Hirokazu Osako

In addition to his work as a poet, he is one of Japan's leading educators. Currently serving as the principal of Kaijo Junior and Senior High School.

Published works include *Gakkou* (2012, Kamakura Shunju Sha), *Teigi Izen* (2017, Yugyosha), *Komorebi* (2019, Message Design Center), and many others.

Graduate of the University of Tokyo.

Asuna Osako

Translator, Poet's daughter.

Psychotherapist in private practice. gentledepththerapy.com

Resides in NYC. Graduate of Columbia University School of Social Work.

ST

Poems Hirokazu Osako

Translated by Asuna Osako